The Birthday Bear

The Birthday Bear

By Antonie Schneider

Illustrated by Uli Waas

Translated by J. Alison James

North-South Books

NEW YORK · LONDON

For Mimi, Anna and Josi   A.S.

Copyright © 1996 by Nord-Süd Verlag AG, Gossau Zürich, Switzerland.
First published in Switzerland under the title *Der geburtstags-bär*.
English translation copyright © 1996 by North-South Books Inc.

First published in the United States, Great Britain, Canada,
Australia, and New Zealand in 1996 by North-South Books,
an imprint of Nord-Süd Verlag AG, Gossau Zürich, Switzerland.

Distributed in the United States by North-South Books Inc., New York.

Library of Congress Cataloging-in-Publication Data is available.
A CIP catalogue record for this book is available from The British Library.
ISBN 1-55858-655-5 (TRADE BINDING)
1 3 5 7 9 TB 10 8 6 4 2
ISBN 1-55858-656-3 (LIBRARY BINDING)
1 3 5 7 9 LB 10 8 6 4 2
Printed in Belgium

For more information about our books, and the authors and artists
who create them, visit our web site: http://www.northsouth.com

Every summer David and his older
sister Sally visit their grandparents in
the country. They live where there are
mountains and rivers, old forests—
and bears!

This year Sally and David arrived on David's seventh birthday.

"Granny," said David, "for my birthday I want a big cake, and I want to spend the night in the tent and go fishing with Grandpa."

"Certainly," said Granny.

Granny's house was on a hill at the foot of the mountains. It was built entirely out of wood. Behind the house Grandpa had his workshop. But most of the time he sat down by the river and fished.

When the children saw him, they ran down the hill to the water, shouting, "Grandpa, will you make us fishing rods?"

Then Grandpa went whistling up the hill to his workshop and made a pair of fishing rods.

And Sally and David ran right back
down to the river.

Later Sally and Granny put up the tent.
David wasn't allowed to help because it
was his birthday treat. So he just lay back
in the noonday sun and watched.

That afternoon Sally and David played
on the bank of the big river.

Grandpa came down the river road on his bike.

"Hello, children!" he called.

With a loud war whoop David burst out of the bushes.

Grandpa had to brake sharply.

"Don't move!" cried David, and he swung his tomahawk. "Indian territory!"

"Oh, I see," said Grandpa. "You're right, you know. All the land around here used to belong to the Blackfoot Indians."

"Are there any Indians now?" asked David.

"Sure," said Grandpa.

"And do they wear headbands with feathers like ours?"

"Some tribes wore headbands with feathers a long time ago," said Grandpa. "Now most Indians dress just like you and me."

"For my birthday let's all wear feathers like those long-ago Indians," said David.

"Okay," agreed Grandpa. He took a piece of fishing line, tied it around his head, and stuck in a duck feather. "How do I look?"

"Great!" said David.

Grandpa got back on his bicycle and waved good-bye.

David and Sally ran back to the tent.
Granny was busy decorating the cake.

Suddenly David remembered the Indian
book that he'd been reading. He tried to
recall what had been happening last. . . .
The Indian boy, Little Crow, had his camp
set up on the riverbank, when suddenly a
bear . . .

"Granny, Granny!" cried David. "Have you seen the book about Little Crow?"

"No, my dear. Where were you reading it last?" Granny replied.

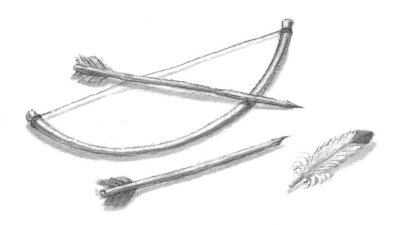

David ran to his usual hiding place—
under the old table. There was the book!
He quickly crawled in and started reading
about Little Crow.

"Your legs are sticking out. I can see
you!" called Sally. She spread a cloth over
the table.

"Shut up," growled David.

Sally always teased David when he was
reading. She was pretty old, thought
David, but she didn't understand a thing
about reading. And certainly not about
Indian adventure books.

"Little Crow, watch out for the bear!" whispered David. Arrows flew through the air around Little Crow.

David couldn't put the book down. He was so deep in the story that he didn't notice Sally putting the birthday cake on the table. He didn't even notice the fine new fishing rod from Grandpa.

Granny stood in front of the tent and looked out at the woods.

"Where is Grandpa?"

"Here he comes now!" cried Sally, pointing at a dark figure in the distance.

Suddenly Granny stiffened.

Sally was scared. She wanted to scream, but Granny held her mouth closed and pulled her behind the tent.

Sally couldn't believe her eyes. A shaggy brown figure came right up to them and stood on its hind legs.

It was a bear!

He came straight to the table.

David was still underneath it, lost in his book.

Sally put her hands over her face.

"For heaven's sake, don't move, David," whispered Granny.

But David didn't hear.

The bear swiped at the birthday cake
and licked the sweet icing off his paw.
He did it again and again until he had
devoured the whole cake.

He stood up and sniffed to the left.
Then he sniffed to the right.

Granny held her breath.

The bear fell back on all fours, ambled down to the river, and swam across.

"The bear is gone!" cried Granny.

Sally ran to her brother and pulled him out from under the table.

"What's wrong?" asked David, surprised. Then he saw the birthday cake.

The tiny flags that had been stuck in
the cake lay all over the place. A bit of
cake stuck to the fishing rod.

"Sally!" cried David angrily. "You ate
my cake!"

Just then Grandpa arrived. "Hey, did
you see that bear over there?" he called.
"What bear?" asked David.
Sally showed Grandpa the birthday
cake. "He got here before you did,
Grandpa!" she said.

Grandpa was astonished. Then Sally and Granny told him what had happened.

"So reading is good for something," laughed Grandpa.

"It can even save your life," said Granny.

"David was lucky," said Sally. "Maybe he survived because it was his Birthday Bear!" She licked the last crumb of cake from the fishing rod.

"I'm as hungry as a bear," said Grandpa. Everybody laughed.

Grandpa had brought a huge fish. He handed it to David. "Here's a real Blackfoot Indian birthday present," he said. "We can roast it on an open fire."

"Oh, great! At least the bear didn't get this!" cried David.

"Come on, Sally," Granny called. "We'll make a new birthday cake."

Sally shrugged. "Okay, but let's eat it right away before a bear gets it!"

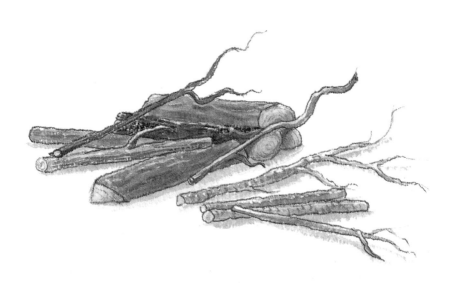

This is a true story. It happened almost exactly the way I've told it. And if you don't believe me, you'll have to go to the mountains yourself. But watch out—not all bears are birthday bears!

About the Author

Antonie Schneider was born in
Mindelheim, in southern Germany.
She has worked as an elementary-school
teacher, written a book of poetry, and
traveled widely. She lives with her
husband and three children in an old
house with a garden that has run wild—
with visitors, housework, books, and
stories (both true and imaginary).
She has written one other book for
North-South, *You Shall Be King!*

About the Illustrator

Uli Waas was born in Donauworth, Bavaria. She studied painting and graphics at the Academy of Graphic Arts in Munich. Since then she has illustrated many books for children, including three other easy-to-read books for North-South: *Where's Molly?*, *Spiny*, and *A Mouse in the House!* She lives with her husband, daughter, and son at the edge of the Swabian Alps.

About the Translator

J. Alison James was born in California. She makes her permanent home in Vermont, but recently spent a year in Norway. She studied languages and got a master's degree in Children's Literature so that she could write and translate books. She has written two novels and translated over thirty books for North-South.

A NOTE TO PARENTS

Reading Aloud with Your Child
Research shows that reading books aloud is the single most valuable support parents can provide in helping children learn to read.
- Be a ham! The more enthusiasm you display, the more your child will enjoy the book.
- Run your finger underneath the words as you read to signal that the print carries the story.
- Leave time for examining the illustrations more closely; encourage your child to find things in the pictures.
- Invite your youngster to join in whenever there's a repeated phrase in the text.
- Link up events in the book with similar events in your child's life.
- If your child asks a question, stop and answer it. The book can be a means to learning more about your child's thoughts.

Listening to Your Child Read Aloud
The support of your attention and praise is absolutely crucial to your child's continuing efforts to learn to read.
- If your child is learning to read and asks for a word, give it immediately so that the meaning of the story is not interrupted. DO NOT ask your child to sound out the word.
- On the other hand, if your child initiates the act of sounding out, don't intervene.
- If your child is reading along and makes what is called a miscue, listen for the sense of the miscue. If the word "road" is substituted for the word "street," for instance, no meaning is lost. Don't stop the reading for a correction.
- If the miscue makes no sense (for example, "horse" for "house"), ask your child to reread the sentence because you're not sure you understand what's just been read.
- Above all else, enjoy your child's growing command of print and make sure you give lots of praise. *You are your child's first teacher — and the most important one. Praise from you is critical for further risk-taking and learning.*

— Priscilla Lynch
Ph.D., New York University
Educational Consultant

For Dr. A.D. Shapiro
who helps kids fight germs
— B.K.

To all the wonderful people
at Shepherd of Peace Preschool
— S.B.

Special thanks to Dr. Lawrence Golub for his expertise.

Text copyright ©1996 by Bobbi Katz.
Illustrations copyright ©1996 by Steve Björkman.
All rights reserved. Published by Scholastic Inc.
HELLO READER, CARTWHEEL BOOKS, and the CARTWHEEL BOOKS logo are registered trademarks of Scholastic Inc.

Library of Congress Cataloging-in-Publication Data
Katz, Bobbi.
  Germs! germs! germs! / by Bobbi Katz; illustrated by Steve Björkman.
    p. cm. — (Hello Reader! Level 3)
  Summary: Rhyming text describes how germs attack the body to cause illness and how careful people make life difficult for germs.
  ISBN 0-590-67295-9
  1. Bacteria—Juvenile literature. 2. Viruses—Juvenile literature. [1. Bacteria. 2. Viruses.]
  I. Björkman, Steve, ill. II. Title. III. Series.
QR57.K38 1996
616'.01—dc20   95-33066
                                                                   CIP
                                                                    AC

20191817161514   0 1/0

Printed in the U.S.A.

First Scholastic printing, November 1996

GERMS! GERMS! GERMS!

by Bobbi Katz

Illustrated by Steve Björkman

Hello Science Reader — Level 3

SCHOLASTIC INC. Cartwheel BOOKS®

New York Toronto London Auckland Sydney

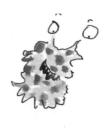

We're on the ground.
We're in the air.
We're GERMS
and we live everywhere!

Can you see us?
Not a hope!
You'll need to use a microscope!

We're so small we can't be seen.
But we are strong and we are mean.

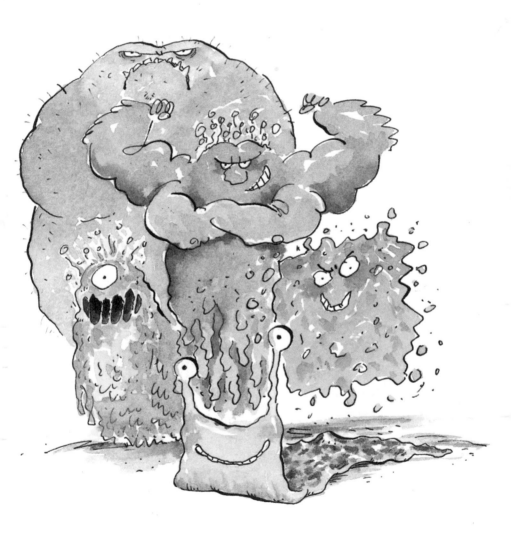

Knock-knock, body. Let us in!
We'll make you sick once we begin!

Every germ thinks it's just grand
to hop in a mouth on a dirty hand.

A tummy ache?

A cold?

The flu?

We can give them *all* to you.

We're on the ground.
We're in the air.
We're GERMS
and we live everywhere!

Give us someplace dark and damp.
What a perfect place to camp!

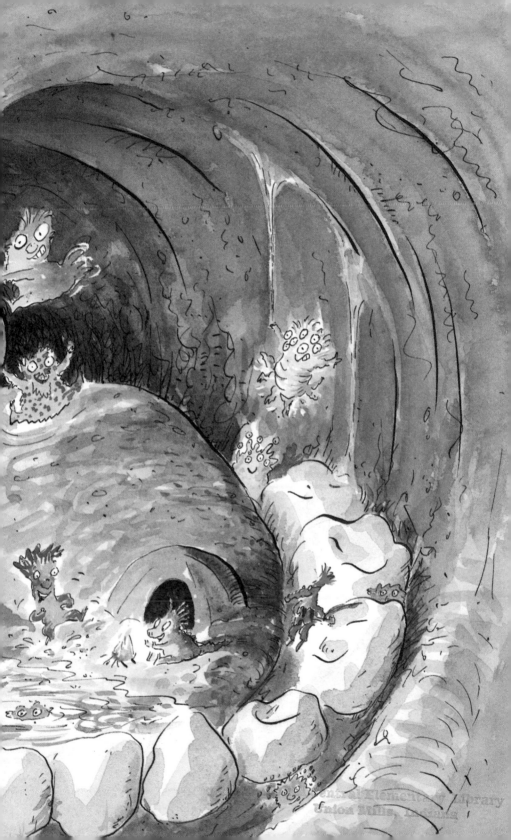

If it's warm, we'd love to stay
and multiply by night and day.

Knock-knock, body.
Let us in!
We'll make you sick
once we begin!

It's not always easy to spread disease.
Germs have lots of enemies!

Hot soapy water — what a curse!

Fresh air and sunshine — even worse!

Some folks we meet are very mean.
Rub-Dub-a-Scrubbers keep
everything clean!

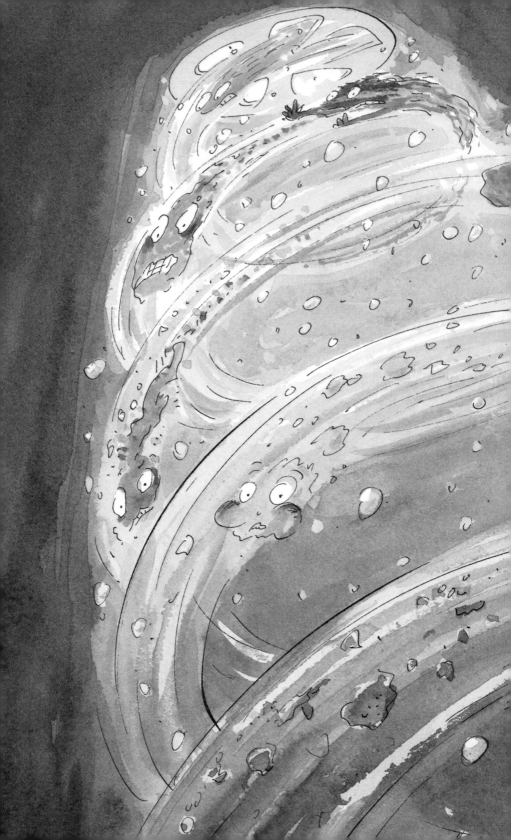

Poor germs like us get washed away.
Then we don't have a chance to play.

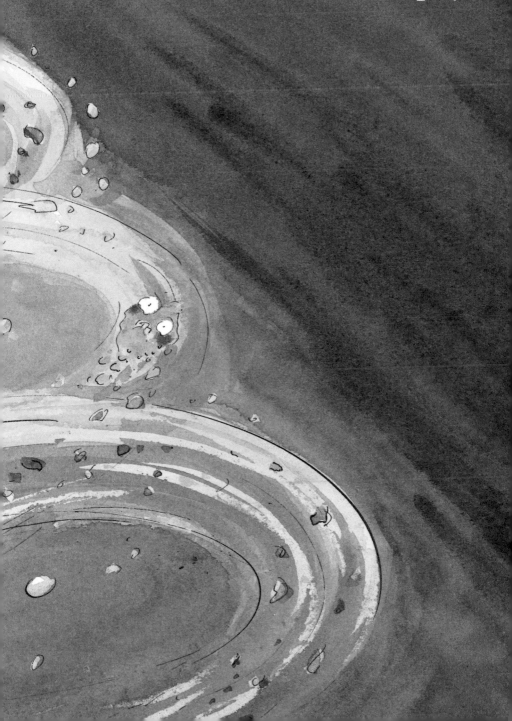

Food-Put-Awayers!
Another bad bunch!
They won't let us grow
in your supper or lunch.

Into the fridge go milk, butter, and meat.
How can we get into the food that you ea

Stop it! Stop it! Hey, you guys!
Leave out something for the flies!

Brushes, brooms, mops, detergent—
let's leave, germs. It's getting urgent.

We can't live here.
But we don't care.
We're GERMS and we go everywhere!

But germs have helpers.
Yes, we do!
Hear that cough and that *kerchoo*?

n winter, people crowd inside.
'hat's when germs get an easy ride.
neezers and Coughers, don't take care!
Ve'll be glad to help you share.

When bodies are tired and get a chill,
will cold germs attack them?
Yes, we will!

We're on the ground.
We're in the air.
We're GERMS
and we live everywhere!

Hurry-Ups help us.
Rush! Rush! Rush!
They're too busy to wash and flush!

Germs like Hurry-Ups so much better
than some careful Never-Forgetter!

Hey, see that kid? Now watch him fall.
Are we sorry? Not at all.

His elbow's cut! He scraped his knee!
Let's go, germs! We'll have a spree!

Open skin has no protection!
We can cause a fine infection!
Hip-hip-hurrah for lovely dirt!
Sorry, kid. Infections hurt.

Who else helps germs? Do you know?
Nose-Picker!
Pencil-Chewer!
Ho, ho, ho!

inger-Licker! Meal-Skipper! YESSIRREE!
Germs have good friends, as you see!
We may have lots of enemies.
But we'll do fine with friends like these!

We're on the ground.
We're in the air.
We're GERMS
and we live *everywhere!*